WAY TOO MANY LATKES

A Hanukkah in Chelm

For Uncle Nat, with
boundless gratitude for
all the laughs and love
we've shared. –L.G.

To my ever-supportive
wife and our little girl.
–A.Z.

KAR-BEN PUBLISHING
A division of Lerner Publishing Group, Inc.
241 First Avenue North
Minneapolis, MN 55401 USA
1-800-4-KARBEN

Website address: www.karben.com

Main body text set in Abadi MT Std Regular 15/20.
Typeface provided by Monotype Typography.

Library of Congress Catalog-in-Publication Data

Names: Glaser, Linda, author. | Zolotic, Aleksander, illustrator.
Title: Way too many latkes : a Hanukkah in Chelm / by Linda Glaser ; illustrated by Aleksander Zolotic.
Description: Minneapolis : Kar-Ben Publishing, [2017] | Summary: "When Faigel can't find her latke
   recipe her husband asks the rabbi, whose advice leads them to make way too many latkes, in this
   Hanukkah story about the foolish people of Chelm."—Provided by publisher.
Identifiers: LCCN 2016028303| ISBN 9781512420920 (lb : alk. paper) | ISBN 9781512420937
   (pb : alk. paper)
Subjects: LCSH: Che?m (Lublin, Poland)—Juvenile fiction. | CYAC: Hanukkah—Fiction. | Jewish
   cooking—Fiction. | Rabbis—Fiction. | Jews—Poland—Chelm (Lublin)—Fiction.
Classification: LCC PZ7.G48047 Way 2017 | DDC [E]—dc23

LC record available at https://lccn.loc.gov/2016028303

Manufactured in the United States of America
2-44696-23235-8/18/2017

WAY TOO MANY LATKES

A Hanukkah in Chelm

LINDA GLASER

illustrated by ALEKSANDAR ZOLOTIC

KAR-BEN
PUBLISHING

In Chelm, the village of fools, Faigel makes the best latkes. But every Hanukkah, she only makes a tiny batch. If you're lucky, she serves you one little latke. And you dream about it for the rest of the year. Except for one year where everything went awry . . .

It was the first night of Hanukkah.
"I don't remember my latke recipe!" cried Faigel.
"How will I make potato latkes?"

"Well, you always use potatoes," her husband Shmuel remembered.

"But how many?" she wailed. "Was it three or maybe four?"

"I'll go ask the rabbi," said Shmuel.

"The rabbi?" cried Faigel. "What does he know about making latkes? Bupkes! Nothing."

"But he's the wisest man in Chelm!" said Shmuel. "He knows more than you think."

"Well, maybe you're right," said Faigel. "Quick. Go ask."

Shmuel ran to the rabbi's house in two flicks of a goat's tail. "Rabbi, help! Faigel can't remember her latke recipe! How many potatoes should she use?"

The rabbi's stomach gurgled. He hadn't eaten much all day. "Tell her to use them all."

Shmuel scratched his head. "Are you sure?"

"Are these my feet?" The rabbi pointed.

"Of course!" said Shmuel.

"Are you sure?" asked the rabbi.

"Sure I'm sure!" said Shmuel.

"Well," said the rabbi, "I'm just as sure about the potatoes. On Hanukkah, that's what potatoes are for."

"You are so wise!" said Shmuel and rushed home.

"The rabbi says to use them all," he said to Faigel.

"All of them? Is he sure?" asked Faigel.

"Are these the rabbi's feet?" Shmuel pointed.

"What?!" cried Faigel. "Shmuel! Where's your head?"

"Right here." He tapped it. "Don't ask silly questions.
Let's just do what the rabbi says."

So Faigel grated all the potatoes—down to the very last one.

Then she clutched her head.
"Oy! With all these potatoes, how many eggs should I use?"

"I'll go ask the rabbi," said Shmuel.

He raced over in two snaps of a chicken's beak.
"Rabbi, help! How many eggs should Faigel use for
the latkes?"

The rabbi thought for a moment. His stomach rumbled.
"Use all the eggs you've got."

Shmuel scratched his head. "Are you sure?"

"Is this my nose?" The rabbi pointed to his nose.

"Of course!" said Shmuel.

"Are you sure?"

"Sure I'm sure!"

"Well, I'm just as sure about the eggs. On Hanukkah, that's what eggs are for."

So Shmuel ran back home. "Use all our eggs!"
"What?!" cried Faigel. "Is he sure?"

"Is this the rabbi's nose?" Shmuel pointed to his nose.

"What?! Have you lost your head?"

Shmuel felt it. "No. It's right here. Let's start cracking eggs."

So Faigel cracked all the eggs—down to the very last one. "Done!" Then she groaned. "Oy! But how many onions should I use?"

"I'll find out." Shmuel ran to the rabbi's house in two flicks of a mule's ear.

"Onions?" The rabbi tugged his beard. His stomach grumbled. "Use all the onions you've got."

Shmuel's eyes bulged. "Are you sure?"

"Is this my head?" The rabbi pointed.

"Of course!" exclaimed Shmuel.

"Are you sure?"

"Sure I'm sure."

"Well, I'm just as sure about the onions.
On Hanukkah, that's what onions are for."

Shmuel ran home. "The rabbi says use them all."

"Oh my goodness!" Faigel threw her hands in the air.
"Is he sure?"

"Is this the rabbi's head?" Shmuel pointed to
his own head.

"What?!" cried Faigel. "My husband doesn't even know his own head anymore! What next?!"

"Onions!" exclaimed Shmuel.
"Don't you remember? Let's start chopping!"

So Faigel started chopping. She chopped and chopped . . .

Then she fried up the latkes. Up to her elbows. Up to her armpits. Up to her earlobes. And each latke was a crispy golden masterpiece.

"Done!" She wiped her hands on her apron. Then she held her head. "Oy! We have too many latkes! If we eat all these latkes, we'll get bellyaches up to our eyeballs."

Shmuel nodded. "I'll go ask the rabbi what to do."

He raced over in two shakes of a cow's tail. "Help, Rabbi! We have way too many latkes!"

"No!" The rabbi shook his head. "There is no such thing as too many latkes." He held up his finger like a true sage. "Just not enough mouths."

"Very wise," nodded Shmuel. "But Faigel and I have only one mouth each."

"Ahh." The rabbi's stomach growled loudly. "Don't worry. I can help. I'll come to your house, and I'll bring my mouth with me."

But when they got to the house, the rabbi shook his head. "I can't eat all these latkes—not even if I stuffed my mouth from now until the last night of Hanukkah."

"Oy!" moaned Faigel. "What will we do with all these latkes?"

The rabbi stroked his beard. "There's only one answer. We need more mouths."

"More mouths?" Shmuel felt around his face for more mouths.

The rabbi shook a finger at him. "Not *our* mouths! Go! Invite the whole village. Quick, while the latkes are still hot. Tell everyone to bring one mouth each. On Hanukkah, that's what mouths are for."

And so Shmuel did. The whole village rushed over to help solve the problem of too many latkes.

And—oy!—did they help! On Hanukkah, that's what a village is for.

There were just enough mouths and just enough latkes, down to the very last one.

A NOTE ON CHELM STORIES

Do you want to know how Chelm came to be? Well, an angel had a sack of foolish souls to scatter around the world. But, as luck would have it, the bag got too heavy and all the souls spilled out into the small Eastern European village of Chelm. While there is a real Polish town called Chelm, the fictional Jewish town has become a beloved part of Jewish folklore. Stories that take place in this "village of fools" are full of silliness but also sprinkled with a bit of wisdom. The first stories of Chelm were written in Yiddish in the late 1880s. Since then, Jewish writers have continued to entertain readers with stories about the citizens of Chelm who are famous for their ridiculous problems and their often equally ridiculous solutions.

ABOUT THE AUTHOR

LINDA GLASER is the award-winning author of over 30 children's books including the Sydney Taylor Award-winning *Hannah's Way* and Reading Rainbow featured book *Our Big Home, An Earth Poem*. In addition to teaching and writing, she conducts writing workshops for schoolchildren and adults. She lives in Minnesota.

ABOUT THE ILLUSTRATOR

Award-winning illustrator **ALEKSANDAR ZOLOTIC** graduated from the Faculty of Applied Arts in Belgrade, in illustration and animation. Variety of style gives him the chance to work on comic books and video games in addition to children's books. He enjoys drinking ice coffee and eating homemade muffins with his wife and showing picture books to his baby daughter. He lives in Serbia.